CRULLER ME SURPRISED

RAISED AND GLAZED COZY MYSTERIES,
BOOK 16

EMMA AINSLEY

SUMMER PRESCOTT BOOKS PUBLISHING

CHAPTER ONE

Maggie Sharpe drove her car along the lower lake road, close to the shores of Dogwood Mountain Lake. She found the perfect spot, a grassy area close to the water, and pulled her car into the dirt parking area on the side of the road.

"You don't think that's too close, do you?" her only son, Bradley, asked her. He had traveled north to visit her from his post in Oklahoma where he served as a naval liaison. His son, Wyatt, chattered and cooed in the car seat behind her. Each tiny noise he made had Maggie grinning harder.

"He's not going to get close enough to the water before you or I can get to him," Maggie said. "It's not like he's crawling miles at a time or anything." She was familiar with the worries that came with being a parent and enjoyed seeing her son experiencing them.

"Fine. You grab Wyatt and I'll get the picnic basket," Bradley said. "It was nice of Aunt Ruby to fix up such a feast for us."

"You really like calling her Aunt Ruby, don't you?" Maggie asked as she pulled the baby from his seat.

Ruby Cobb was her best friend and business partner at Dogwood Donuts. As far as she was concerned, Ruby and the other members of their small crew was all the family she needed. It warmed her heart to hear her only child find a kinship with her new family, too.

"I do." Bradley smiled. "She's closer to me than anyone else on your side of the family. Dad's too, for that matter."

"You're not spending time with your dad?" Maggie was careful not to say too much about her ex-husband in her son's presence.

"He still hasn't even met Wyatt, Mom," Bradley said.

Maggie was silent for a moment. The last thing she wanted to do was cross wires with her son about her former husband. Since the divorce, he was no longer her problem and that was just fine with her.

But she still didn't like hearing that he wasn't available for their son and grandson.

"You know, that absolutely breaks my heart for your dad," she said, holding the baby close to her chest. "If he only knew what he was missing out on."

Wyatt snuggled against her and placed a chubby baby hand on her face. "If he only knew what he was missing," she whispered as she cradled the small boy against her.

Bradley headed toward the grassy area with the picnic basket and a blanket. Maggie reached into the back for the light umbrella stroller. She opened the stroller with one hand and secured the lock with her foot. She told herself she still had it, handling a stroller with a baby on her hip was both as easy and difficult as she remembered it to be.

Maggie wheeled Wyatt down the slight hill and stopped short of where her son had spread the blanket. She knelt on the blanket and reached into the picnic basket. She pulled out two boxed lunches and an extra small box with "Wyatt" written on the top. Maggie smiled and peeked inside. She found a small container of applesauce, a tiny portion of well-cooked rice, and a bit of sweet potato with butter. Ruby had added a few slivers of chicken as well.

"It's a good thing he likes food," Bradley said.

Maggie smiled. She made a mental note to thank Ruby for the adorable child-friendly meal. "I'm sure he will love everything. He's such a good eater."

Bradley settled down on the blanket across from her. They took turns feeding the baby as they ate their lunch. Maggie was glad she had taken the day off for a picnic by the lake. Bradley was due to return to the base in a couple days and this was their last day of fun before life returned to normal.

"I have some news to share with you," Bradley announced about halfway through their meal.

"You've been here an entire week and now you decide to share news with me," Maggie said. "What is it? What's wrong?" Her motherly instincts kicked in and she almost laughed at her dramatics.

"This is good news," he said, shaking his head at his worried mother.

"I'm listening," Maggie said. She offered a bite of sweet potato to Wyatt and smiled as he messily ate it.

"I've put in for my terminal leave," Bradley said. "I'm thinking about coming back up this way at the end of the summer to look for work," he said. "Specifically, I'm lining up interviews in Joplin."

"Hold on," Maggie said. She unstrapped Wyatt from his stroller and set him on the blanket next to her.

"You're leaving the Navy? I thought the plan was to stay in until you had twenty years."

"Gee, Mom. I thought you might be a little more excited for me," Bradley said.

"Oh, I'm ecstatic! I'm just shocked that you're getting out," Maggie said. She picked the baby up and kissed his chubby cheeks. "Joplin is so close to Dogwood Mountain! What kind of work are you looking for? I can ask around if you think it might help."

Bradley smiled and shook his head. "Slow down, Mom," he said. "I appreciate the offer, but I'd like to try to do this on my own. I don't want to feel like I'm riding your coattails or something. I've been looking for an I.T. position. I have a terrific resume from the Navy, and I'll have some help with buying a house."

"I can't believe it," Maggie said. She shook her head and pulled little Wyatt onto her lap. "Maybe Mimi should take some time off from the donut shop to come up and take care of you." She kissed her grandson on the top of his head.

"No, Mimi needs to stay where she is and let me handle childcare," Bradley said. "I want you to just be Mimi, not the babysitter. And it would be nice to have a place to go on the weekends when we want to come home."

"Deal," Maggie said. "You boys can come home any time you want to. I can't believe you're going to move so close." She was so proud to see him making these decisions.

"I'm going to look for the possibility of working from home and in the office," Bradley said. "That way I can spend more time with Wyatt."

They spent the rest of the afternoon playing with the baby and looking on their phones at neighborhoods in Joplin that Bradley thought he might move into.

Maggie stood up and stretched her arms over her head. "I'm going to have to find my way to the restrooms soon," she said.

"That's okay," Bradley said. "I think it's about time for this guy to take a long nap anyway." He strapped Wyatt back into the stroller and folded the blanket up. Maggie picked up the remainder of their lunch and packed it into the picnic basket. She followed him up the hill to the car and handed over her keys.

"Just drive around to the other side of the lake and you'll see the restrooms," Maggie said once they were all in the car. They rounded the lake and pulled in close to the campsites. Bradley pulled the car onto the road between the campsites and the R.V. parking.

"What is that?" he asked and pointed toward the area behind the women's restroom.

"Looks like a bunch of trash," Maggie tsked.

"Looks like somebody had a party here last night," Bradley said. "A lot of somebodies."

"I'll let the police department know when we head back home," Maggie said.

"You mean you'll call your chief of police boyfriend?" Bradley teased her.

"Yeah. That still sounds so weird to say, though," Maggie said. She blushed at his reference.

"You two could always get married and that way you won't have to refer to him as your boyfriend anymore." Bradley shrugged, seemingly satisfied with his brilliant solution.

"That's enough of that. We are fine just how we are." Maggie scrunched her nose and swatted at her son's arm. He was getting as bad as Orson and the rest of the crew at the donut shop.

"Could have fooled me," Bradley sang to his little son in the rearview mirror. Wyatt cooed and giggled as though he knew just what was going on.

Maggie shut the car door and rolled her eyes. She wasn't against the idea of marriage, but it wasn't a topic of conversation either. She moved past the trash, eyeing it carefully and thinking about what a shame it was to see, and headed straight into the restroom.

"Oh, gosh," she said out loud when she entered the bathroom. The smell of something rotten nearly overtook her. Her full bladder prevented her from running straight back to the car. She covered her mouth, ran into the closest stall, then washed her hands as fast as she could.

She stepped out into the fresh air and let out her breath. But the wind had shifted. The stench came from just outside the bathrooms. Maggie walked around the side, careful not to step in the debris. She pulled the sleeve of her light windbreaker over her hand and covered her mouth again.

"That is so gross," she said. She moved around the back of the pile closest to her. The grass was covered in discarded alcohol bottles, cans, and dozens of cardboard boxes. She spotted takeout bags from three different restaurants, including some from Hunter Springs and others a good twenty miles from town.

Maggie stepped around the side of the building where more trash littered the side. Some trash was even up against the wall. She shook her head but stopped short of heading back to the car. Something about the pile of trash seemed off to her. She stepped in a little closer, careful to avoid the trash around her feet, and walked ahead a few feet.

"Oh, no," she said and pulled her cell phone out of her back pocket. She snapped a photo of the pile of trash, sent it to Brett's phone, and then called him.

She guessed from the pair of shoes and the discolored hand poking out from the trash pile that the body had been there for more than a couple of days.

CHAPTER TWO

Brett Mission pulled his police cruiser to a stop behind Maggie's car. He opened the door and stepped out into the heat of the day, which appeared to hit him along with the putrid smell of trash and death. Maggie noticed the look on his face and knew just how he felt.

"Wyatt and I will see you at home," Bradley called from the driver's seat of his mother's car. Maggie waved at the fussy baby in the backseat. Brett had asked her to stay for initial questioning and while he wanted Bradley to be there too, there was no way they could keep Wyatt around something so awful.

"See you." Brett waved to both of the Sharpe boys as they pulled out of the small area and onto the main lake road.

"I hope you don't mind running me back home when we're finished here," Maggie said. "I can always have Ruby pick me up if it's better."

"We'll work it out one way or another," Brett assured her. "I'll still need a statement from Bradley at some point, but I saw no reason to keep the little man from his nap. And, well, most normal people want to get as far away from a potential crime scene as they can."

"Except us."

Brett groaned and nodded. "So, tell me again what happened. Step by step."

Maggie started at the beginning. She told him about when they arrived, what they ate, and even the good news from Bradley about moving closer to Dogwood Mountain. When she moved on to finding all the trash and then the body, Brett held up a hand.

"I'm sorry. I want you to know that I'm not trying to be callous or anything." Brett frowned. "I noticed the look on your face when you were telling me about Bradley and Wyatt moving closer. I had to stop you to let you know that I'm thrilled by the good news. I want to make sure we celebrate this. Just not now."

Maggie smiled. "Oh, please. I totally understand. I wasn't trying to share the news, you just asked me to go step by step and that's what I did."

"Okay, keep going." Brett looked relieved all of a sudden. It was always strange to have to separate the horrors of work with the real life stuff.

Maggie led him around to the back of the bathroom structures and around the trash to the other side but made sure to stay far enough away from the body. "The odor hit me before I even went into the bathroom," she said. "I ran inside and used the facilities and then came back out and followed the trash around to the other side." She pointed to the pile of trash. She covered her mouth again when they stepped closer.

"Oh, boy," Brett said when he saw the hand.

"Do you think the body is male?"

Brett tipped his head side to side. "By the size of his hand, I would guess that," he said. "But the medical examiner will be here soon to make that determination."

"What do you think happened here?" Maggie asked. "A party gone wrong, maybe? I'd hate to think this one person could consume all of this alcohol and junk food by themselves."

"Unless that's what did him in," Brett said. He looked up and nodded to Brooks Macklin who had just parked his own police cruiser behind the chief's car.

"About time you got here, Macklin," Brett teased.

"I got held up. There's lots of drama downtown at the market. Some sort of coupon fraud and the manager isn't having it," Brooks said. "What's going on here?" He eyed Maggie.

"I'll fill you in," Brett said. He pulled on a pair of surgical gloves and turned to Maggie. "Do you mind…"

"Not at all," she finished, already knowing he was going to ask her to step away while they worked. "I'll be by the lake."

Maggie took the opportunity to walk along the shoreline. She decided it was a good time to feel the breeze off the lake, anything to help get the smell of trash and death out of her nostrils. As she walked, her phone rang.

"Hello," she said.

"Maggie, Bradley called me and told me what happened," Ruby said on the other end. "Are you doing alright?"

"I'm fine," she said. "Brooks is here with Brett looking over the scene and taking photos now. I decided to treat myself to another walk down by the lake while they take care of things."

"How did the picnic go otherwise?"

Maggie relaxed at the change of subject. "Those

sweet potatoes were a hit, but that's not even the best news. It seems Bradley is planning on leaving the military so he can find a job in Joplin," she said, barely able to contain her excitement.

"Are you serious?" Ruby said. "So, he's getting out of the Navy?"

"He thinks it would be the best way to continue to raise his son," Maggie said.

"I'm so happy for you and him." Maggie could hear the genuine happiness in Ruby's voice.

"Me too. But what's going on with you? It's been so busy at work lately that we've hardly had any time to talk. When is your town hall meeting?" she asked.

"It's more of a meet the candidates forum and it's Friday night at City Hall," Ruby said. "Oh! Did I tell you that two other candidates dropped out this week?"

"You didn't. So, that means it's down to you and two other people?"

"Three others, but the polling numbers sure seem to point to just two of us," Ruby said. "And I have a slight edge over Lois Turnbill."

"She hasn't lived here long, has she?" Maggie asked.

"I understand she moved up this way from

Charlton City three years ago. Since then, she has started at least four different businesses," Ruby said. "I don't know what she actually does for a living."

"What businesses does she have?" Maggie asked. She could see some movement out of the corner of her eye. She turned her back to the scene up the hill and kept walking, this time in a new direction. She noticed a man and a woman under a tree about thirty feet from her. She smiled at first, seeing how happy they looked having their picnic, but then frowned, realizing they had no idea what was going on in the distance.

"Lois has dabbled in real estate, timeshares, dog breeding, and she sells some high priced cosmetics to anyone who will listen to her for longer than two seconds," Ruby said. "And I still have no idea where her money comes from."

"Has she tried to sell you cosmetics?"

"She has." Ruby laughed. "Beware. She will definitely make her way to you soon enough."

Maggie swore she heard a vehicle behind her. She turned in time to see the medical examiner's white van driving up to meet Brett and Brooks. "Looks like the cavalry has arrived," she said to Ruby. "I better go and see if the police chief is ready to take me home."

"If not, you call me," Ruby said.

"I know, you or Myra or Orson." Maggie laughed.

Maybe she was the one with the calvary.

CHAPTER THREE

A few hours later, Brett popped his head through Maggie's open office door. "I've got about thirty minutes; would you like to grab a quick bite to eat with me?" he asked her. "I wouldn't mind a blue plate special from Flo's food truck."

Maggie smiled. She could use a bacon, lettuce, and tomato sandwich from The Diner, the small food truck that was parked in the donut shop parking lot beneath her highway sign. Flo Johnson, the truck's owner had quickly become a close friend to both of them.

"Well, I haven't heard a thing from Bradley, which makes me think he decided to take a nap along-side his son," she said, considering the idea. "Sure.

Let's go grab something to eat. We can bring it back here and eat in peace."

"Deal," Brett said.

They ordered their food after waiting in line behind a single woman and then a family of five. Thankfully, Flo was quick and efficient and before they knew it, they'd returned to Maggie's office.

"It's no picnic." She shrugged. "But neither was the one I attempted to have earlier…"

"It's perfect. Like I said, I don't have very long before I have to get back to work, but Brooks has things covered while I eat. Plus, I wanted to check in with you." Brett looked at her carefully. "How are you?"

"I'm okay," Maggie said as she got herself settled at her desk. "I'll make sure Bradley gets down to talk to someone about his statement. I can even head out of here early to keep an eye on Wyatt if I have to."

"It'll be fine. I can always stop by your house to talk to him. He's not a suspect, just a witness and he's barely one at that." Brett cut into his hot roast beef sandwich with his fork. "And unfortunately, this guy isn't going anywhere." He paused. "That came out wrong. I'd love for him to get up and walk away, but sadly, that's not going to happen."

"So, it is a male?" Maggie asked, understanding that Brett hadn't meant to be harsh.

Brett nodded his head. "I think that's safe to say," he said. "You aren't going to give the newspaper a scoop on this, are you? I hear we've got a tabloid reporter running around this town and I'm doing everything I can to avoid being part of whatever nonsense they think they can stir up."

Maggie looked at him and rolled her eyes, wondering what on earth a tabloid reporter would want in Dogwood Mountain. It was hardly grounds for anything newsworthy with no famous people anywhere around. "Of course, I am. It's first on my list of things to do when you leave. In fact, are you almost done?"

"Yes, the victim is a male," he said, ignoring her horribly dry sense of humor.

"Victim? So, we're talking about a crime here?" she asked.

Brett nodded and pushed a forkful of mashed potatoes into his mouth but chewed them slowly. "He didn't die of natural causes."

"It's tragic either way, but I was sort of hoping this wasn't another murder," Maggie admitted.

"Well, it's up to the M.E. to determine officially,"

Brett said. "But the big gash in his forehead might be a clue to a cause of death."

"Oh no," Maggie said. "Do you think he was murdered there or moved afterwards or what?" She shuddered thinking about having just been there with her son and grandson.

"I don't know those answers quite yet," he said. "But with all of that trash and debris around him, it sure looks like there was a party that went the wrong way. And then whoever he was with just abandoned him."

"Or that's the way it was supposed to look..." Maggie said.

"What do you mean by that?" Brett asked as he pushed the food around in its container.

"I mean, it almost looked too convenient, don't you think? There was so much trash all around him," Maggie said. "Didn't it sort of look like somebody just stood back and threw the trash at him?"

Brett said nothing. Instead, he nodded his head and sipped his iced tea. "That's a very good point," he muttered at last. "You don't think it's possible they had a party, and everything just happened that way? You know how some young people can be, completely ignorant to where they're leaving their stuff. Add a whole bunch of alcohol and you have zero consideration for anyone else."

"Okay, tell me this, then," Maggie said. She sipped her own sweet tea and inhaled deeply before she began to speak.

"I'm listening." Brett slid his food out of the way and sat forward a bit in his chair. He leaned his arm on the desk.

"First of all, why were all of the alcohol containers in a pile along with the fast food trash? Who eats and drinks alcohol all at once and throws the trash in a small area? Most parties I've ever been to require a whole lot of moving around and goofing off, not sitting still. And last but not least, who in the world drinks themselves into oblivion and eats fast food outside of a bathroom in the middle of a huge park by a big lake? Where and when did they even get the fast food? Most of those restaurants are nowhere close to Dogwood Mountain!"

"Are you finished?" Brett asked her, looking at his food.

"Have I made my point yet?" Maggie asked.

"Yes, loud and clear." Brett chuckled.

"Okay," Maggie said, her lip curling. "That's all I had to say."

He shook his head. "You make good points and as you know, I'll look into every last one of them."

"But will you tell me if I'm right?"

Brett tilted his head. "How about we just finish eating and go from there?"

"Right, but I really think there's more to this than what it looks like," Maggie said as she dipped an extra-long fry into a pool of ketchup.

"And you're probably right about that." Brett sighed. "Believe it or not, I don't love eating while we talk about this sort of thing. I commend you and your strong stomach, but I'm not cut out for this kind of conversation while I have food in front of me."

Maggie laughed. "Eat. I'm sorry. I just get worked up easily and feel like I have to talk everything out all at once."

"Trust me, I know." He winked and dug into his sandwich with a smile on his face.

CHAPTER FOUR

"I heard the good news," Myra said when she came into the donut shop kitchen the following morning. "Bradley and the baby are moving to Joplin!"

"Bradley is looking for work in Joplin," Maggie replied. She was excited but trying not to get her hopes up yet.

"Yes and who knows, maybe he can find a remote position and live even closer," Ruby said with a wink. "Oh, by the way, I have a request from the Hunter Springs Day School for about five dozen boxed lunches. They specifically requested peanut butter and jelly donuts along with one of our typical dessert donuts."

"Please don't tell me they requested a donut for the entrée." Maggie cringed.

"No, but they want me to cut the donut in half and use it in place of bread," Ruby said. "But don't worry. I'm more than making up for that with fresh veggies and some fruit. These kids are going to love ants on a log and apple slices before their picnic is over."

"What's ants on a log?" Myra asked. "Please, please tell me that isn't some weird delicacy with actual ants."

"Oh, my sweet summer child," Ruby said and embraced the younger woman. "Ants on a log is a childhood classic. It's literally peanut butter spread on celery sticks with raisins on top. Get it? Ants on a log!"

"Oh, thank goodness!"

"You girls sure do gab a lot," Orson Howard, resident curmudgeon and adopted father to all of them, said when he poked his head into the kitchen through the swinging door. "Ruby, there's a group of ladies out here wanting to speak with you. I recognize two of them as locals, but the others haven't lived here long. Good luck."

"What now?" Ruby mouthed. Since the announcement of her candidacy as a member of the city council at large, more than one person had come by the donut shop to have a word with her. Recent polling showed that Ruby was the most favored to win, which meant people were flocking to her like crazy.

"Can I help you?" Ruby asked. Maggie followed close behind her. She had a new tray of chocolate glazed donuts to add to the display case and decided to make herself busy while Ruby dealt with the public.

They had an arrangement. While she was running for city council, Maggie would hang around close by in case the conversation got out of hand. Ruby had gone out of her way to provide members of the public with access to her. She met weekly for coffee with people who wanted to talk over the issues with her. She had a special phone number for people to call and leave messages, and she returned each and every phone call within one day. She kept her social media profiles open, too. But the one request she made was that no one come to Dogwood Donuts during business hours. However, it didn't always happen that way.

Most citizens respected her request, but a few, like the four women staring back at her from across the counter, didn't care about her request. They were quite convinced that her time belonged to them. Maggie was thankful she had decided not to pursue the council seat herself. Ruby was built for such inter-actions. As an executive chef in her earlier life, she had plenty of experience dealing with emotional people. Maggie, on the other hand, could be professional but it was much easier for her to lose her cool.

"We would like to talk to you about what happened at Dogwood Mountain Lake yesterday," one of the women said. She stepped forward from the group and appeared to be the spokesperson. Each woman seemed to be somewhere in their forties and each one was a version of an unnatural blonde. They also all had the same look on their faces: narrowed eyes, stretched neck, and pursed lips.

"I assume you're talking about the body that was found," Ruby said quietly. "Why don't you ladies come to the coffee chat with me first thing in the morning? That would be the more appropriate setting for this type of discussion."

"Of course, we're talking about the body that was discovered out there! We need to talk about what this means for our safety!"

"What is your name, ma'am?" Ruby asked quietly.

"You ought to know my name," the woman snapped. "I have left you plenty of messages and spoken with you several times."

"I recognize your voice, but not your face," Ruby admitted.

"My name is Tanya Clemmons," she said.

"Okay, yes, Tanya." Ruby smiled and nodded her head. "The thing is, I'm at work right now and this isn't the right time or place to discuss these matters. Especially if you can't do it quietly."

"Oh, you will discuss this with us right here and right now! We deserve that time from you," Tanya said. Her voice seemed to rise with each word she spoke.

"You know, my business partner may not appreciate us discussing such things while her customers are eating," Ruby said. "If you want to take a seat, I can chat for a few minutes, but not here and not like this."

Maggie heard the first comment and moved in. It was her secret code to get involved. She approached the counter and moved slightly in front of Ruby.

"Ladies," she said softly. "I am going to have to ask you to either sit down and be my guest to a cup of coffee and discuss these matters a little more quietly or you're going to need to wait until Ruby leaves the donut shop for the day."

"We have every right to talk to our city council members whenever and however we want to," Tanya said. "I'm not going to tolerate serious things being made to look trivial. I had enough of that in the last place I lived."

Maggie sighed. "Actually, you can't have access to anyone twenty-four hours a day. You all know that. I understand why you want to speak with Ruby even if she isn't an official city council member yet. Heck, she's my best friend and my business partner on top of it. I wish I could vote for her ten times over instead of just once. But this is her workplace. She is more than happy to spend about twenty minutes with you over coffee, which again, will be on the house. But a discussion up here at the counter isn't going to work."

"I could go for one of those cinnamon lattes," a woman to Tanya's right said.

"Be quiet, Sasha!" Tanya flipped around and whispered fiercely at her. Maggie recognized the woman from the line at the food truck.

"One cinnamon latte coming right up," Myra said behind them.

"What will you have?" Maggie asked one of the other ladies behind Tanya. She quickly received their orders and turned back to Tanya. "You're the only one left. What can I get for you?"

"I'll try the brown sugar cinnamon cappuccino," Tanya said begrudgingly. "I would like a large one."

"Okay," Maggie said with a smile. "Why don't

you pick out a place to sit and we'll bring these out to the four of you as fast as we can? Ruby will join you soon."

Tanya gave her a half smile and led the pack to a far table.

"Thank you," Ruby whispered. "That one is a tough nut to crack."

Maggie decided to take over running the front while Ruby held her short meeting with the women. She heard some of their comments and was prepared to step in with an emergency in the kitchen if Ruby gave the code phrase. She didn't feel a bit guilty or deceitful for the arrangement. Ruby had made more time for her potential constituents than any of the other candidates.

"We need something to be done about the crime in this county," Tanya said as soon as they were seated.

"I know there are problems everywhere," Ruby said. "But remember, as a potential future member of city council I can only affect what's happening here in Dogwood Mountain, not the county at large. You want to speak with the county commission about those issues, too."

"I'm here speaking to you," Tanya said. She glanced over at the counter where Maggie was busy rearranging donuts in the display case. She raised her voice slightly. "And I know full well that you have a special audience with the chief of police, too. So, what is he going to do about this?"

"Well, the lake is actually under the county's jurisdiction," Ruby said. "But the Dogwood Mountain P.D. has a special agreement to patrol the lake for the county. The sheriff's department will follow up on their investigation."

"Okay, fine, but what are we going to do about the fact that there was another murder out there?" Tanya asked.

Maggie decided to join them. "I don't know if you heard, but I'm the one who discovered the body," she whispered. Tanya and each of the other women immediately scooted forward in their seats and leaned over the table. "I was the one who called the police first."

"What did you see?" Sasha asked her.

"At first, just a bunch of trash," Maggie said. She lowered her voice like she was telling a huge secret. "Then I saw a hand... a discolored hand."

"What else did you see?" Tanya asked. She was completely taken in as well.

"Really, just a lot of trash," Maggie said. She chose her tone as if she was telling state secrets, even though she merely repeated herself. "But I don't know if I can say anything else. I have to be careful."

"Right," Tanya said. "That makes sense."

"And listen," Maggie said. She leaned over and patted Ruby's arm. "One thing I love about Ruby's campaign is the fact that she doesn't care who is in charge. She's all about transparency, and she's not loyal to one party line over another. It's all about Dogwood Mountain."

The conversation turned to Ruby's campaign after that. Maggie stood and excused herself quickly. She left everyone at the table smiling and talking in normal tones. Ruby rose from her seat a few minutes later and Maggie heard the approving words from the women.

"You really turned that one around for me," Ruby said when she walked back into the kitchen. "That Tanya Clemmons is a fire-breathing dragon."

"She is a force to be reckoned with," Maggie said. "What are you going to do with her if you get elected?"

Ruby shrugged and smiled. "I am going to ask her to become part of a neighborhood watch group. Someone like that is a diamond in the rough."

CHAPTER FIVE

Maggie gathered the pile of Wyatt's clothes that she'd just folded and set it on top of the spare bed where Bradley had placed their luggage. She smoothed a small blanket with her hand and blinked back the tears she wanted to shed.

Maggie fought off the tears through the rest of the morning while Bradley loaded his small son and their things in his car. He promised to call her with the dates he would be back in town in a matter of a few weeks. She told him she would take off work to keep Wyatt while he searched for a new job. He promised her he'd figure it out on his own, but she wouldn't take no for an answer.

Shortly after, as her boys drove off, Maggie waved until they were well off into the distance. She wiped away the tears she'd no longer been able to contain, and quickly got herself ready and to the donut shop.

"And if you can't get away for some reason, Wyatt can spend the day with me out at the farm," Ruby said when Maggie arrived at work and told her everything.

"And if Ruby is too busy on the farm, Wyatt can come and hang out with me at my house," Myra offered.

Orson shuffled the clean towels in his hands. He stared at the rest of them. "Fine," he said. "If all of the women folk here are too busy, Wyatt will spend the day with his Papa Orson."

Jake Jenkins, the youngest member of the donut shop crew, looked up and held his hands out. "Don't any of you look at me! I'm not good with kids, babies especially!"

Myra burst into giggles, followed by Maggie and Ruby.

"I'm serious," he said and hurried through the swinging door and into the dining room like a team of babies were chasing after him.

Maggie walked across the kitchen and draped her arms around Orson's neck. She kissed his cheek softly and patted him on the back. "I love the sound of 'Papa Orson,'" she said.

Orson said nothing but hugged her back. Maggie was sure she saw him wipe a tear from his eye, and even more sure she noticed a slowing in his step. He had already cut his hours back to just a few a day and had begun coming in later in the morning.

"I think we really need to have that talk, Maggie," Ruby whispered to her. They had discussed hiring another person to help run things throughout the day. With the election looming, Orson slowing down and spending more time with Gretchen, Myra talking about starting a family, and now Bradley moving back into the area with Wyatt, Ruby argued that it might be a good time to discuss hiring a manager.

"Fine," Maggie said, much louder than Ruby's whisper. "I know you're right. We need someone who will be here day in and day out to help run things when one of us might have to leave."

Myra hovered over a tray of chocolate cake donuts. She dipped her spatula into the cherry flavored frosting and paused. "Hang on a sec," she said. "Are you guys talking about hiring a manager for this place?"

"Well," Maggie said, frowning at herself for being so loud. "Orson cut his hours back again. It's looking more and more like the election is going to go in Ruby's favor. I'll be here but when Bradley moves back it's likely that I will have to be a backup for Wyatt if his sitter is sick. It just makes sense."

Myra set the spatula down and folded her arms over her chest. "Why don't we just hire another worker and you all let me do what we talked about before?" she asked. "Why are you passing me over?"

"Oh, Myra, we aren't passing you over," Ruby spoke up. "You've been talking so much about having a baby sooner rather than later, we just assumed your time would be more precious, too."

"Why don't you ask me what my plans are?" Myra said. "The truth is, Brooks and I have discussed it at length. We plan to hire someone to care for our baby after she is born. Brooks usually starts work a couple of hours after I do, so he can take her to daycare. We will love our future baby, but we can still love our jobs, too."

Maggie glanced at Ruby. "And you've already planned this all out? This will work for both of you?"

"We have and it will," Myra continued. "And I would like to talk to the two of you about being here to open but take off around noon every day. That's quite perfect if you ask me. I can work through the morning and be with her for the rest of the day."

"And you are quite sure this future baby will be a girl?" Orson muttered from the storeroom.

Myra ignored his comment and turned back to Maggie. "Honestly, another pair of hands would be nice around here, but only to help us out. He or she could close each day and work on the weekends."

Ruby nodded her head and nudged Maggie. "Look at this one, getting all smart on us and everything."

Maggie nodded. "You are absolutely right, Myra. We did make the deal to have you take over more responsibilities, didn't we? I am sincerely sorry for assuming what you might want to do when you start a family," she said. "So, two things. One, why don't you call the paper and put in an ad for a new employee? You can handle the initial interviews and Ruby and I will take over for the final interview."

"Okay, on it," Myra said with a smile. "Now, what's the second thing?"

"The second thing is, just when were you planning to tell us? How long have you known?" Maggie asked.

"How long has she known what?" Orson asked.

"You're not saying what I think you're saying," Ruby spoke up.

Maggie looked at Myra and folded her arms expectantly. "Well?"

Myra blushed, stood up, and pushed her stool under the baker's table. She turned to the side and smoothed the front of her loose-fitting apron over her still flat stomach. "Brooks and I have known for a little while."

"What?" Ruby moved quickly across the floor to embrace her. Maggie followed. Orson remained in the storeroom and beamed.

"Don't you think I already knew?" he asked at last. "Why do you think I have been cutting back some of my hours? I'm going to help out with the baby, too. I can come in a little later in case Brooks has an emergency at work."

"Orson, you are too sweet," Myra said. "I hadn't even thought about that possibility."

"You knew and didn't tell us?" Maggie grimaced but her smile was back right away. There was no chance she could be mad.

"Well, when you and Brooks decided to make an apartment for me in your new house, I decided then and there I was going to help out in any way I can, for as long as I can," Orson said.

"You know, I think we ought to look at hiring two new people, both part-time, to help cover any gaps in the hours," Maggie said. "We certainly could do it."

"I agree completely," Ruby said. "Then we can consider expansion."

"Expansion?" Maggie and Myra asked in unison.

"I've been thinking about Hunter Springs," Ruby said. "This isn't the time to bring it up, but I think we ought to look into running the food truck up that way a few days each week. Consider it a test run. We might decide to open up a second location before it's all said and done."

Maggie winked at Myra and smiled. "Sounds like that newspaper ad better include one full-time and one part-time position," she said. "And it might be a good idea to get it into tomorrow's edition."

"I'll make the phone call now," Myra said. She started for the office.

"Oh, no you won't," Ruby said. She shoved another stool at her. "First things first! How far along are you? When is your due date? Have you started thinking of names? How will you decorate the nursery? Who will be in the delivery room? Oh, what about a baby shower? I have so many ideas for food." Ruby stared at the group like they were slowing her down. "What are we doing just standing here? I've got work to do."

As she rushed off, Maggie heard Ruby listing off food ideas.

"Bacon skewers, veggie cups. Ooooh! Marshmallow rattles, and deviled eggs turned into tiny baby carriages…"

"I think she's excited," Maggie said.

"She's definitely something," Myra teased.

Orson strolled into the kitchen with his hands on his hips. "I say she's a few deviled eggs short of a dozen…"

CHAPTER SIX

Maggie left work a little early and headed straight for the restaurant supply shop in Joplin. Ruby wanted to join her, but when her farmhand informed her that one of her cows was close to calving, she had to beg off and leave the errand to Maggie alone.

While she drove, Maggie decided that she'd drive around the town of Hunter Springs before going home. It wasn't that expansion hadn't been on her mind; it was merely the fact that her mind had been filled with many other things. "Maybe," she thought, but then dismissed it immediately. Bradley wanted a career in technology, not running a second brick and mortar location of the donut shop.

When she arrived at the store, she went straight in and began searching for a high-backed stool with a foot rest for Myra. She was determined to find ways to make the pregnancy as easy as possible. After she selected the best stool, Maggie shopped around for a bit longer and found everything she needed much quicker than she'd expected.

Her cell phone rang as she headed back out to her car. "Where are you?" Brett asked her when she answered the phone.

"Hello to you too. I'm in Joplin," she said. "I had to make a run for some supplies."

"Right, hello." Brett cleared his throat. "I'm guessing you've already heard the happy news. Brooks just now told me."

"And? Are you upset?" She couldn't read his tone over the phone.

"No! Not at all," he said with a chuckle. "I did tell him some pointers for raising daughters if that's what they end up having. But no, I am very happy for them. By the way, when do you plan to be back in town? I'd like to see you tonight."

"I'm headed back now," Maggie said, suddenly feeling concerned. "I should be there in about forty-five minutes."

She dismissed her previous thought of looking around Hunter Springs. She had no right to suggest the idea to her son when he'd already settled on

Joplin and a new job that had nothing to do with running a second location of her donut shop. She had to get the idea out of her head.

"Do you care if I stop by? Or do you feel like Italian? We haven't been to Curley's in quite a while."

"Italian sounds great," Maggie said. "But you have to give me fifteen minutes to change out of the clothes I'm wearing."

"Deal," Brett said. "But I can do even better than that. I'll see you in an hour and a half."

Maggie called Ruby next and told her about the stool and her finds at the store. She decided to drop everything off at the donut shop before making her way back home. She pulled into the alley behind the donut shop, and it only took her a moment to unload the new stool and a few bags.

"Hello? Are you the owner of this place?" a male voice called from behind her. Maggie turned to see a strange man standing in the middle of her kitchen. He was tall, well over six feet, if she had to guess. His hair was black, and it stood up in thick shocks on top of his head. Maggie focused on his piercing blue eyes.

"Why are you here? Who are you?" Maggie shouted her questions. She could feel the panic rising in her chest.

"Hold on, I mean no harm," the man said. "My

name is Victor Larabee. Faylene Larabee is my aunt and I'm here in town about the bookstore."

"She never mentioned you," Maggie said, thinking of her sweet friend who had recently decided to move away from Dogwood Mountain. Faylene had moved to Wisconsin and the last time Maggie spoke to her was the week before. She told her about a last-minute cruise that she and a new friend were taking. If Maggie remembered correctly, they had set sail the day before. It made no sense for her to send her nephew to town while she was gone, but of course, Maggie had several reasons to be paranoid of strangers, even the most well-meaning.

"I'm not surprised that she didn't," Victor said. "I haven't spoken with my aunt in many years. She and my father had quite a falling out. It surprised the heck out of me when she called me and told me that she wanted me to take over the bookstore. I just went through a messy divorce so moving down here to the Ozarks seemed like the next best thing to do."

"How can I help you?" Maggie asked. She was quite unsure what he was doing there in the first place. It wasn't exactly that she felt threatened, but she did not like his presence.

"I can't seem to get in touch with her, but she did tell me about a good friend of hers who lived here.

Unfortunately, I didn't recall the name she gave me so imagine my luck when I stopped by the bookstore to check it out and ran into a very helpful local who knew all about you."

"You got into the bookstore?" Maggie asked. None of it made sense. There was no way he'd have a key to the place.

"Oh, no, no. I was just browsing around the outside, and checking out the town," Victor explained. "I wanted to make sure that I'd fit in here before I agreed to anything."

"I see. Well, I'm not sure how I can help. I think it's probably best for you to wait and talk to your aunt."

"Yeah, I thought that too, but it seems she's gone on a trip or something. I can't seem to get in touch with her no matter how hard I try. I just have a few questions is all, and who better than a friend of hers and a citizen of this charming little town?"

The more Victor spoke, the more Maggie had to wonder about him. Faylene never mentioned a nephew or a brother for that matter, but if Victor was telling the truth and there was a falling out, that made sense. She knew her friend was on a trip, which was why he couldn't get in touch with her and without a cellphone, it, too, made sense. Perhaps with the move and the sudden cruise, Faylene had overlooked telling her about the possibility of someone taking over the bookstore.

Deciding to give the guy the benefit of the doubt, Maggie agreed to help him where she could.

"Why don't you stop back here tomorrow morning at about ten, Victor? We can have coffee and discuss whatever it is that you want to know."

"Oh, well, I had hoped to take you out to dinner tonight," Victor said.

"She already has a date for tonight," Brett announced from the doorway. He looked past Victor at Maggie. "I drove by here on the way to your house and saw your car. I'm glad I stopped."

"I got delayed, but I'm ready to head back home," Maggie said, relieved to see Brett. She turned to Victor. "Why don't you stop by in the morning like I suggested? We can talk about Faylene, and I'll tell you what I know about the bookstore."

"Will he be here?" Victor asked. "Because I'm not so sure I want to stop by if he is."

"Just who are you, and why are you standing here in the kitchen of a business that's closed for the day?"

"Why do you want to know?" Victor snapped. "I've already explained to Ms. Sharpe who I am and why I'm here. You aren't her stalker or something, are you?"

"Brett is the chief of police," Maggie said. She was getting agitated by the stranger's attitude. He might be her friend's nephew, but she felt quite put off by him. "And the reason I cannot go out to dinner with you. We are a couple."

"So, you see, I have two good reasons for asking you questions," Brett said.

"Okay. Then are you asking me as her boyfriend or as the police chief?" Victor asked.

"Both," Brett said firmly. Maggie felt a thrill climb up her back. Brett's words and tone had an unexpected effect on her.

"I'm out of here," Victor said. "I will see you here tomorrow." He walked out the door and stopped short of shouldering Brett as he passed him.

"What in the heck was that all about?" Maggie asked after he left.

"I was going to ask you the same thing," Brett said. "Did he just show up here? Have you ever met him before?"

"Never seen him before in my life," Maggie said. "He just appeared while I was putting things away. He says he's Faylene's nephew and that he might take over the bookstore for her."

"Did you know anything about that?" Brett asked.

"Not a thing, but it could be true. I know she didn't want the bookstore to go to some stranger who would run it into the ground. I just think it's odd she never mentioned him in general, never mind a quick call to tell me he was coming. She's not much for spontaneity."

Brett pondered her words. "Normally, I'd agree with that, but she did just up and decide to leave town out of nowhere. And didn't you say she was going on a cruise with some guy she just met?"

"I'd hardly call being attacked by a crazed killer 'out of nowhere'. And she's not going with some guy she just met." Maggie rolled her eyes, exasperated. "The local community center where she lives has these events a few times a year. There was an opening and her male neighbor told her about it."

"Close enough." Brett shrugged.

"Not really at all, but either way, I'll do what I can do to help this guy and don't think I'm not counting down the days until she gets back on land. The first thing I'm going to do is tell her she needs to invest in a cellphone and better communication skills."

"I'll never understand why everyone doesn't have a cellphone in this day and age. No matter how old or young you are, they're just part of life. Maybe I should consider having a class about the importance of it in regard to personal safety," he trailed off. "Anyway, do you want me to follow you home or do you want some time to change and stuff first?"

"Of course, I still want you to follow me home." Maggie grinned. "I won't take any time at all to change, and we then can get going to Curley's."

Brett followed Maggie out of the donut shop and waited while she locked the door. He looked around to make sure Victor was long gone. Satisfied, he walked her to her car and didn't move a muscle until she was safely inside.

CHAPTER SEVEN

Brett opened the door to the Italian restaurant and waited while Maggie stepped inside. True to her word, she'd run home and emerged freshly dressed in less than ten minutes. She'd smiled to herself at Brett's reaction to seeing her.

"Would you like to have a seat on the patio, sir?" a waiter asked when they stepped inside.

Brett looked at Maggie. "Do you want to sit outside? It's a lovely night," he said.

Before Maggie could answer, thunder cracked outside. Lightning lit up the interior of the restaurant and Brett and Maggie laughed together. "I think that just answered your question."

They were led to a booth in a somewhat secluded section. Maggie was grateful for the privacy. She settled into her seat and ordered a glass of red wine. Brett ordered an appetizer and waited while Maggie looked through the menu.

"I think we'll just start with the appetizer," he said. "We might need a few minutes to choose an entree."

The waiter nodded and left them alone. "What sounds good to you?"

"It's been a while since I've been here," Maggie said. "Everything sounds good to me."

"I think I'm going to stay with a classic," Brett said. "Lasagna."

"I'm going to order the seafood ravioli," Maggie said finally. She folded her menu over and informed the waiter when he returned with her glass of wine.

"So, what do you think about that Victor guy?" Brett asked her when the waiter left them again.

Maggie shrugged. "I think he needs a lesson in manners. Who just walks into a place of business after hours and does that? He scared the heck out of me."

"I don't like the guy at all," Brett said. "I don't care who he is or who he is related to."

"Are you saying I shouldn't meet with him tomorrow? I think I can sit down with him for a few moments and see what he has to say," Maggie said.

"I'm not going to tell you that you shouldn't meet with him," Brett said. "I would never try to tell you what to do. Not unless I knew someone was a dangerous criminal or something."

"Speaking of criminals, has anything else happened with the body at the lake?" Maggie asked.

"We don't have an identity just yet, if that's what you're asking," Brett said. "He had no identification with him, but he did have a couple of tattoos that might help. But so far he doesn't match up with any active missing persons reports."

Maggie nodded. "I've heard a few stories about people being identified because of super specific tattoos. I hope that's that case here."

"I'm afraid the ostrich tattoo on his arm and the window tattoo on his chest aren't going to prove very helpful," Brett admitted.

"What about the medical examiner's findings?"

"He definitely ruled it as a homicide," Brett said. "He couldn't pin down an exact time of death, but we had a look at the trash that was scattered all around and it sure seems like that trash was placed there. The food was aged at different rates, too. If that makes sense."

"In other words, chances are the trash was just

thrown there and not part of anything the victim actually consumed," Maggie said.

"Basically, yes," Brett said. "The fact is, I think somebody just took some trash out of the trash cans and threw it on top of him."

"That's my best guess based on what we know right now, anyway," Brett said. He stopped speaking and looked around. Although their voices had been low and quiet, the few people within earshot of them appeared to have stopped to listen.

"Do you think they heard us?" Maggie whispered.

Brett shrugged his shoulders. "I thought we were being very careful," he said. "I don't know how anyone could hear what we were talking about. Maybe they're just not used to seeing us out together."

Their waiter appeared with the appetizer. Maggie nodded when he offered her a second glass of wine. She was going to enjoy herself, although she had no plans to drink too much wine. Brett ordered a light beer for himself. Maggie knew from experience that he would be careful not to drink too much, especially not in public.

"I still can't believe Myra and Brooks are going to have a baby," Brett said after a bit. "I mean, not only does it make me feel very old, but it also makes me extremely happy that someone has found the love of their lives. They have a such bright future ahead of themselves."

Maggie smiled. "I couldn't agree more," she said. "It makes me hold out hope for…"

"I hope you're going to say for yourself, Maggie," Brett said earnestly.

"I was actually going to say it gives me hope that Bradley and little Wyatt might find someone else to share their lives with," she said, blushing deeply.

A shadow fell over their table before she could speak. Maggie looked up at a red-faced Tanya Clemmons, the woman who had been at the donut shop earlier in the day to speak with Ruby. Brett looked up at her as well. He glanced at Maggie and shook his head as if he was confused by the woman's presence.

Tanya folded her arms and turned toward Brett. "Is this really an appropriate use of your time, Police Chief Mission?"

"I beg your pardon," Brett said. "I don't think we've met."

Tanya reached across the table and picked up Maggie's wine glass. "Oh, this is rich," she said. "Our very own chief of police is out here drinking in public while we have a murderer on the loose!"

"Excuse me," Brett said. He rose from his seat

and removed the glass from her hand and set it back down hard on the table. "Who do you think you are?"

"That's my glass anyway," Maggie said, though she wasn't sure her words actually went anywhere. "What do you want, Tanya? You're interrupting our dinner."

"Why is the police chief out rubbing shoulders with you when there is a crisis in this town? Why are you out here with him instead of letting him be so that he can do his job and keep this town safe?" Tanya asked. Her volume increased with each word she spoke. She looked over her shoulders for reactions.

Another voice rang out from across the dining room. Maggie strained to see who it came from. "That's a very good question," the woman's voice said. "I would like to have an answer to that question myself. I would like to know why the sheriff is not in his office right now working on this case. I'd also like to know why an elected official is not working on a murder case and is out to dinner with some woman instead."

"Some woman?" Maggie rose up out of her chair and turned toward the speaker as Brett tried to reason with Tanya.

"Sit down, Sasha!" Tanya spat.

She glared at Tanya and looked as though she was

going to back down but kept going. "No, I demand to know why you aren't out there trying to find the person responsible for the death of the young man at Dogwood Mountain Lake, Chief Mission," Sasha shouted again. "Because it looks very bad for you to be here."

"Is there a problem here?" The maître d' appeared in the middle of the dining room. Maggie sat back down abruptly.

"My companion and I were enjoying dinner out, and this woman came over here and started shouting at me," Brett said. Maggie was shocked at his calm demeanor. Her fists were still balled at her sides and ready to swing.

"Ma'am?" The host waited for an explanation from Tanya.

"I think I have made my case known," she said. "I could ask you why you would serve alcohol to an officer on duty!"

"I am not on duty," Brett said coolly. "And I would appreciate it if you would mind your own business and let me get back to mine. I am the chief of police. And the investigation into the mysterious death at the lake is well in hand."

"If that's the case, why are you here?" Sasha

shouted from across the restaurant. Tanya shot her a look that could kill.

"Okay, that's it," the host said. "All of you, out! You will remit your bills with the cashier up front and leave here at once!"

"Looks like your date is over, Chief." Tanya smirked.

"Not them," the host said. "You! And your loud-mouthed friend over there in the corner."

"Sasha, if you just got me kicked out of this restaurant, you are really in for it," Tanya snapped. Maggie watched as the restaurant manager joined the host to escort both women and all of their companions from the restaurant.

When the ruckus was over, the manager appeared at the table. "I would like to offer you my sincere apologies for that," she said. "Whatever that was."

"I wish I knew," Brett said. "Maybe one of them is the tabloid reporter and they're just after a story."

"They came into the donut shop," Maggie explained. "They were a little boisterous then, demanding to know what Ruby planned to do about crime if she is elected to the city council."

"I am so sorry," the manager said again. "I have comped your meals and I would like to offer you both gift certificates for your next meal with us." She set the certificates on the table and apologized again.

"Why does it seem like we can't catch a break?" Brett asked when the manager left.

"What do you mean?" Maggie asked.

"Almost every single time we go out or plan to go out, something crazy happens," Brett said. "Half of our dates were ruined by extraordinary circumstances."

Maggie shrugged. "Are you saying we should stop trying?"

Brett looked shocked. "Of course not. But I am saying that maybe... well, I don't know what I'm saying."

"How about we take our meals to go? We can head back to my house and watch a movie or something while we eat."

He nodded, a little defeated. "Yeah. That will be good."

CHAPTER EIGHT

Maggie stepped into the shower after Brett left for the night. The words of the woman at the restaurant had really bothered her. Was the entire scene a response to their conversation about the body at the lake? She couldn't imagine that anyone had actually heard what they were saying, but she couldn't imagine two grown women interrupting their dinner, either. Not to mention what the other diners had to endure.

She fell into bed with a headache and a desire to punch someone. Maggie was not the punching type, but the desire was still with her the following morning when she woke up to start her day. She had just finished making her coffee when she heard a knock at her door. She rushed through the kitchen to open it, thinking that it might be Jake.

But when she got to the door and opened it, she remembered that Jake had moved into Orson's old house. Victor Larabee stood on the other side of her door. "It's four o'clock in the morning," she blurted out.

"It's actually four-thirty," he said and pushed beyond her into the house.

"How do you even know where I live?" Maggie asked. "And why are you in my house? I haven't invited you in."

"Oh, I thought you just did," he said. "No matter. I'm here now. How about that coffee?"

"Mr. Larabee, you can leave my house right this minute," she said. "It is not okay for you to show up unannounced at four o'clock in the morning."

"Four-thirty," Victor corrected.

"Four-thirty, whatever," she said. "It's an ungodly hour. You are not invited in. You can come back to my place of business at ten o'clock as we discussed yesterday, and I will be happy to sit down with you and have a cup of coffee and discuss your aunt. Until then, do not show up at my house again."

"Your lights were on," he said.

"Yes, because I own a donut shop and we tend to get there early to start the day," Maggie snapped. "That is not an open invitation for perfect strangers to show up at your door and invite themselves in," she said.

"But you're already up," Victor said. "Why can't we talk now?"

"Because I have things to do. I have to get to work and get things going for the rest of my employees. Have you been living under a rock or something?" Maggie asked. "Is there some reason that you don't understand the way normal life works?"

"I still don't understand why we can't just have a cup of coffee and a quick chat!" His fist came down hard on the table. "That's all I wanted, just to talk to you. What's so bad about that?"

"Okay, you're acting very strange, and you're starting to scare me," Maggie said firmly. "I want you to leave my house right now, Victor. Leave and do not show up here again."

Maggie held the door open for him and waited for him to leave. She could feel her heart beating hard in her chest. What if he didn't leave? She wondered if he was dangerous. Her thoughts were interrupted when the glow from a set of headlights filled her doorway.

"Who is that?" Victor asked. He moved toward the door and pulled her out of the way. "What can we do for you, Mr. Police Officer?"

"Oh, no," Maggie said. She looked past Victor and saw Brooks getting out of his police car.

"Brooks," she breathed, grateful to see him. "Come in. Please. Now."

Brooks stepped out of his car and stared at Victor. Maggie was quite aware of how things looked. Victor was answering her door long before the sun was due to come up.

"What is going on here?" Brooks asked at last.

"We were just about to sit down to a cup of coffee," Victor announced. "I would invite you to join us, but this is a two-person kind of thing."

"No," Maggie shouted. "No, we were not about to sit down and have coffee! I want you to leave and never come back!"

"Sounds like you better hit the road, buddy," Brooks said. Victor remained in the doorway.

"Move right now," Maggie said. "Get out of my way and get off of my property."

"I don't think you really mean that," Victor said. "Just what would my dear Aunt Faylene think?"

"Oh, no," Maggie said. "I love Faylene but promise you that I do mean every word of it. Leave. Get out. Get lost. Do not return. Clear enough?"

"Fine," Victor said. He threw the screen door open and let it slam hard against the side of the house.

"You had better watch it," Brooks warned. "You just might end up in the back of a police car."

"Yeah, yeah," Victor said. He threw a look over his shoulder at Maggie and disappeared down the road.

"What on earth was that all about?" Maggie said when he left.

"I thought I was supposed to ask you that question," Brooks said.

"I'm so glad you showed up when you did," Maggie said. "I opened the door thinking Jake was here. And he just pushed his way inside. He is very pushy. And he got angry and hit my table really hard."

"He threatened you?" Brooks asked. His face was suddenly very dark.

"Not with words, but I sure felt threatened," she said. "I want there to be no misunderstanding here. I don't want that guy around me at all."

"Understood," Brooks said. "If you want to file a restraining order against him, we can take care of that today."

"That sounds like a good idea. I don't care if that guy is Faylene's nephew or not," she said. She hugged her middle and shook her head. "Wait, why are you here, anyway?"

"I came to tell you two things," Brooks said. "It has been a very active night and early morning and Brett sent me here to talk to you because he couldn't get away."

"What's going on with Brett?"

"He's fine, but for one thing, we have an identity now on the victim at the lake. His name is Chester Thomas, and he has been missing from his job in Fletcher, New York."

"New York? He came all the way here from New York?" Maggie asked.

"That's what it looks like according to the sheriff's department," Brooks said. "They're more involved now. Actually, they are in charge of the investigation from this point on. They have information that proves he was here on business, but that's all I know."

"So, someone killed a guy from New York, and left him in the middle of the Ozarks?"

"More or less," Brooks said.

"I wonder if it had to do with whatever business he was in?" Maggie asked.

"Like I said, the sheriff has taken over the case and if I had time to dig into the man's business, I would, but that's the other reason I'm here this morning." Brooks sat at the table and motioned for her to join him. "Turns out someone else was killed last night. Or maybe early this morning. The M.E. hasn't given us a time of death on that one yet."

"Oh, my gosh," Maggie said. "Who died?"

"A Tanya Clemmons was found dead in her garage early this morning by her friend, Sasha Lorenzo," he said.

Maggie felt herself fall back a little. "You have got to be kidding me," she said. "I just saw her last night. Oh, gosh." She covered her head with her hands.

"I didn't know you two were close," Brooks said.

"We weren't," Maggie said. "I only just met her, but don't you see? She had two very public meltdowns in a short time. And do you know the one thing both of those events have in common? Me."

CHAPTER NINE

Maggie arrived late to the donut shop. She'd accompanied Brooks to the police station to give her statement about the events from Curley's to another officer, along with information about her encounter with Tanya at the donut shop previously. It was Brooks who suggested she get her statement on record. He suspected that the investigation into the murder might be taken from the police department and given to the county sheriff.

"Brett wants to come by later and take statements from everyone else," Maggie announced when she arrived at last. She apologized again to Ruby for showing up so late.

"Stop it," Ruby ordered. "If you apologize again I'm going to throw something at you."

"Okay, okay," Maggie said. "It's been a rough couple of days."

"I heard about what happened on your date with Brett," Myra said, her hand gently rubbing her stomach.

"What happened?" Orson asked, suddenly hurrying over and looking very concerned.

"I had an unexpected visitor early this morning," she said, skipping over the information about her date. "That guy who said he was Faylene Larabee's nephew showed up at my house and pushed his way inside. He got angry when I told him to leave, and Brooks just happened to show up in time. I want it known that he is not to come around here. If you see him show up, call the police."

"You're terrified of this guy," Ruby said. "I have never heard you sound so adamant before."

Maggie nodded her head. "I am terrified of him," she said. "He wouldn't take no for an answer this morning. And when I said no again, he slammed his fist onto my table. I have no idea what would have happened if Brooks hadn't been there. I filed a restraining order against him as fast as I could."

"Okay, well, if we see him, we'll call the police," Myra said. "No worries." She looked from Ruby to Orson with her eyes wide and wondering.

"Look," Maggie said. "You know how there is always that person in the movies or in a really good book who ignores all of the signs that something bad is going to happen, or that someone is dangerous?"

"And you sit there yelling at the screen for them to listen to you," Myra added. "I know what you're talking about."

"Well, I am determined not to be that person," Maggie said. "I want to be loud and clear. I don't want that guy around me."

At Ruby and Myra's insistence, Maggie spent most of the day working in the kitchen away from the public. Ruby fielded questions from curious members of the public about the death of Tanya Clemmons once the news circulated around town. She directed everyone to the press release sent out by the police department.

When the day was winding down, Maggie made the decision to go home and sequester herself inside for the rest of the evening. Myra had set up interviews with two potential employees for the afternoon. If the candidates were acceptable, Ruby and Maggie would set up another meeting with them and make the final decision.

"Do you want some company tonight?" Ruby asked her. "I was thinking about ordering a good dinner from Flo's. I could bring dinner over to you and visit."

Maggie exhaled slowly. She wanted to choose her words carefully. In one respect, she loved the idea of spending time off of the clock with her best friend. But in another respect, she wanted to be alone. She felt like being alone and that had to be okay.

If she was honest, she was feeling a little sorry for herself. She missed her son and her grandson. She wanted to be far away from anyone who might show up at her door uninvited and wreak havoc in her life.

"Maggie," Myra interrupted. "Are you still with us? You're zoning out a little bit."

"Yeah, sorry," Maggie said. "I'm here. I was just thinking about how I want to spend my evening."

"Maybe I'm being pushy right now, but that absolutely just made up my mind," Ruby said. "I will be at your house around five with dinner. I will text you before I get there so you know that it's me."

Maggie nodded and agreed to have her come over. The decision had been made for her. And it was okay. She might do better with some company for the night. If by some chance Victor Larabee showed up again, it would be nice to have someone else there with her.

"I would love a turkey club and some soup for

dinner," Maggie said when Ruby asked. "Loaded fries might be nice, too."

"Got it," Ruby said.

Maggie headed home just after two. She decided to tackle the spare bedroom to stay busy while she waited for Ruby to bring dinner. She pulled the bedding off of the bed and carried it to the washer. She flipped the mattress and fluffed the pillows. Within an hour, she had the room dusted and vacuumed and completely rearranged.

When she was finished, Maggie carried her laptop into the kitchen and then headed back to the laundry room to move the sheets to the dryer and place the heavy quilt in the washer.

She glanced at the clock when she returned to the kitchen. Ruby would arrive in a little over an hour. She tapped the table with her index finger when she sat down. She felt impatient and frustrated. She looked at her cell phone and stared at the dark screen.

An idea sparked in her head. Maggie turned on her computer and clicked on her favorite search engine. Her curiosity was fired up, but she wasn't sure if she wanted to research new recipes for the donut shop or find out what she could about Victor Larabee.

After about five minutes of debating, Maggie settled on a third option and typed "Tanya Clemmons" into the search bar. She wondered if maybe she was the tabloid reporter Brett had been talking about and perhaps she'd done something over the top and made the wrong person angry. She scanned to the end of the first page of search results and found a link to a blog under Tanya's name. She clicked on the link and read through the description.

"The Town Crier" was the name of the blog. Instantly, Maggie disliked the dark layout and white text. The other main color was red. She had to look away from the terrible color palette several times while she read through the first few posts. Her latest post was titled, "The Insanity of Small Town Life."

"In what is supposed to be a storybook setting, crime and violence has once more come home to roost," the post began. Tanya wasn't much of a writer, but she had a gift for exploiting minute details and inserting her own assumptions and hyperbole. The entire post read like an article from a tabloid from the grocery store, but it was clear she wasn't an official tabloid reporter.

Curious, Maggie scrolled back through the archives. She discovered Tanya's story about the town she lived in prior to her move to Dogwood Mountain.

At one point, she had lived in another small town, this one in southern Kansas. Her rhetoric was much the same. Harleyville, Kansas held all the charms of a quaint hometown. She had used similar words to describe Dogwood Mountain.

Maggie's curiosity soared. She found a few instances of Tanya calling out local officials, including law enforcement, for their inattention to the crime that plagued the small town. She read a particularly caustic post and frowned.

"Today was another one of those days here in the blissful little town we all love. I sipped my coffee at Basic Brew while reading my latest library book. While I sat there, I watched the cars and people passing me by on Main Street. I tried to maintain a sunny outlook, but the glaring problems in this town make it too hard to enjoy a simple cup of coffee on a Wednesday morning."

The post continued to mention a few near-misses between passing cars, several drivers Tanya was sure ran over the speed limit, and a rumored assault near the car wash. All the while, she wrote, the two police officers on duty that day were seated ten feet away from her reading the newspaper and eating donuts in the coffee shop.

"What will become of our charming small town if

the local police department is too busy consuming their beloved carbs to pay adequate attention to the crimes committed right under their noses?"

"Whoa," Maggie said aloud. She picked up her phone when she heard the notification that Ruby had texted her. An hour had passed by as she read through Tanya's blog. A moment later, Ruby appeared at her back door with their supper.

"I have something interesting to show you," Maggie announced when Ruby walked in. She passed a sack to Maggie and followed her into the kitchen.

"I see you have your laptop open," Ruby said with a smile. "Am I to presume that you have been engaging in some unofficial investigating?"

Maggie smiled and pulled her food out of the sack. "I think a little unofficial investigation is better than counting the dust bunnies in my bedroom," she said. "That was my other option."

Ruby pulled a chair from the table and sat down with her food. "Alright, what have you found?"

"A blog," she said. "Actually, Tanya Clemmon's blog. She called it 'The Town Crier' and she used it to air her grievances with the town she used to live in. Looks like she had been doing the same thing since she moved here. And it seems she'd do or say just about anything to get a story."

Maggie turned the laptop screen. They read through a few of the blog posts, especially the posts that called out the police.

"I can't believe she had such a low opinion of the local police," Ruby said. "It sure seems like she was gearing up to do the same thing here."

"Especially last night," Maggie said. "What I want to know is, what in the world motivated her to do it?

"Why call attention to yourself and try to polarize yourself with the rest of the town? Whether here in Dogwood Mountain or back in Kansas, why on earth would you do that?"

Ruby took the mouse from Maggie's side of the table and began to click through the rest of the website. After a moment, she turned the computer back to Maggie. "I think I found her motivation," she said. "She has been trying to publish a book. Actually, several books."

"All about crime in small towns," Maggie said. She examined four poorly made book covers and read the descriptions under each. "She was trying to get someone to pay attention to her work and publish her books. They look very unprofessional, but they appear to be selling okay. Maybe she wanted a bigger reach."

"She obviously had some support," Ruby said. "We saw that when she showed up at the donut shop to demand my time. But it makes you wonder if there were those that did not appreciate her message. I wonder what the comment section looks like."

Maggie took the laptop back and clicked to the post she had read through before. She selected the comment section and sat back in her chair. "That post received over two hundred comments," she said. "And there are a lot of people who didn't like what she had to say. Some of them even talk about how what she has to say is nothing but trash and that she needs to quit writing if she knows what's good for her."

"There are a number of comments about another blogger, too," Ruby pointed out. "I saw a few people mention the name, 'Fearless Fenster' in their comments."

"I saw that, too. And I don't think Tanya cared much for that. I found a few links to another true crime enthusiast who goes by that same name," Maggie said. "And those commenters seem to think this person 'Fearless' is a much better activist than the likes of Tanya Clemmons. But I really have no other information about them, whoever they are."

"'Fenster' is the German word for window," Ruby

said. "Aside from that, I don't know anything, either. "I just thought it was interesting."

Maggie froze. "I don't even want to know why you know that, but how sure are you?"

"About the window thing? A hundred percent. I used to work with a German guy years ago and when a plate was ready to be served he'd scream the word 'fenster' to alert the servers there was something for them to pick up in the food window." Ruby shrugged. "I guess I'd be a good partner for trivia night."

"While that may be true, I think you might have just figured something important out. Chester Thomas, the guy who was found at the lake had a window tattoo. What if he's this Fearless Fenster person?"

"Chester Thomas. Chester. Thomas." Ruby repeated.

Maggie stared at her blankly.

"There's something about that name that sounds all too familiar. Is he from around here?

"No, Brett said he came from New York or something."

"Hmm," Ruby muttered. "So, we think Chester is... was Tanya's rival. But we're missing something since Tanya is dead too, now."

"Right," Maggie agreed. "There's gotta be someone else involved."

CHAPTER TEN

Rain began to fall early the next morning. Maggie rushed out the door to her car, hopeful no one would appear out of the shadows before she could get in and lock her doors. She repeated her behavior at the donut shop and rushed inside the back door.

This was one of the times she wished the food truck in the front opened as early as the donut shop did. She began to set the ingredients out for the batter for the automatic donut machines. Orson had challenged her to create a red velvet cake donut with cream cheese icing. Maggie considered it a little plain for "something new," but it was also a classic and she was determined to put her own spin on it. She added a bit of orange zest to the batter and hoped that it would turn out well.

Ruby arrived shortly after she got the first donut machine going. She set to work making the boxed lunches requested by the Hunter Springs Day School, including her version of a peanut butter and jelly donut. Ruby made a full-size donut similar to the smaller version she had created, then sliced it in half and added natural peanut butter and strawberry, grape, or peach preserves. "It sounds nuts coming from a donut shop owner," she said. "But I wanted to reduce the sugar and increase nutrition where I could."

An hour later, she had the first dozen lunches complete. She assisted Maggie with a batch of regular cake donuts in the second automatic donut machine.

"Did you go down any more rabbit holes online last night?" Ruby asked Maggie while they worked together to frost and decorate the cake donuts.

Maggie bobbed her head side to side. "I might have gone through a few more posts," she said. "And the comment sections."

"A few or a few dozen?" Ruby asked her.

"I plead the fifth on that one," Maggie said. "But I did find something interesting before I fell asleep from sheer exhaustion."

"And probably from eye strain on top of it," Ruby teased. "I hope you didn't find any blatant threats to her life. Then again, maybe it would be a good thing to find that sort of a clue."

"I didn't find any blatant threats, but there were plenty of people who identified themselves as the spouses or significant others of police officers who told her she better watch herself," Maggie said. "But most of those comments came from the town in Kansas and not here."

"If I recall correctly, that was years ago," Ruby said. "I know people hold grudges but what are the chances of someone following her here to Dogwood Mountain?"

"I don't know, but I found a familiar name on the blog in many of the comments," Maggie said. "Sasha."

"Sasha," Ruby said and thought for a moment. "Isn't that the name of the woman she spoke down to when they were here?"

"Sure is," Maggie said. "She was also at the restaurant when Brett and I were there for dinner. And she sounded ridiculous."

"Do you think it is the same woman? I mean, Sasha isn't the most common name," Ruby said.

"Not like Maggie or Ruby, right?" Maggie teased.

"Right."

"Anyway, the commenter was Sasha Lorenzo," Maggie said. "She had left comments for years."

"Was there a photo with the comments?" Ruby asked. "Could you tell if it was the same woman?"

"I think it was, but my eyes were very tired, and the picture was a thumbnail," Maggie said. "I plan to verify it when I get a few minutes later."

Ruby agreed to help her look a little later in the morning. She left Maggie in the kitchen alone and headed up to the front to make sure the trays had been cleaned out of the display case. She carried a tray of freshly glazed donuts with her. Maggie followed with a second tray and stopped cold when she looked up at the windows across the front of the shop.

"Who is out there?" she gasped. The sun wasn't up yet, but she could see the outline of someone staring in the front door.

"I don't know who that is," Ruby said. "But I'm headed back to the kitchen for my cell phone. You need to come with me,"

Maggie could see the head of the person outside come up suddenly. He made eye contact with her and began pounding on the front glass.

"Oh, gosh, Ruby," Maggie said. "It's Victor Larabee."

Victor moved in front of the doors. He pushed

hard on the door and pushed his face against the opening.

"Maggie! You filed a restraining order against me! Why would you do that?"

"You better leave here right now, Victor," Ruby warned. "If you don't get out of here, you will be arrested and put in jail. Is that what you want?"

"Where is she? I want to speak with Maggie right now!" Victor shouted. He gripped the handle of the door and shook it so hard Maggie thought he might break the lock.

"Go away, Victor!" Maggie hid behind the counter and yelled. She was unaware of the crowd that had formed behind her. Jake had come into work along with Myra who had been dropped off by Brooks.

Before Maggie was aware of it, Brooks had called for another officer to join him at the donut shop. He patted Maggie on the shoulder as he walked around her and headed for the front door. Victor Larabee stopped pulling on the door handle and pressed his face against the glass. His eyes widened when he saw the uniformed police officer headed across the dining room toward him. He turned to run but was stopped by a second officer who had come up behind him on the sidewalk.

Brooks approached the door and twisted the lock open. He stepped outside and grabbed the other man's arms, holding him still while the second officer put him in handcuffs.

"Alright, alright," Victor said. "I'll go."

Maggie had to turn away from the scene out in the front of her building. She listened with her eyes pinched shut as Victor pleaded across the parking lot and into the back of the waiting police car.

CHAPTER ELEVEN

"I'm beginning to wonder about this guy," Brooks said at noon. He had returned to the donut shop to eat lunch with his wife. Brett joined him and asked Maggie to sit down with them.

"What did you find out about his criminal record?" Myra asked.

"Not too much," Brooks said. "But I…"

"You what?" Maggie asked, noticing the look Brett gave Brooks.

"No… nothing. He has no criminal record," Brooks said.

"But?" Myra held her face close to his. "Who do you think you're fooling? What aren't you telling us?"

Brooks looked at Brett as if to apologize.

"What is going on?" Maggie asked. "If there's something else going on, I want to know. This guy won't leave me alone and I want to be able to tell Faylene that her nephew is a creep, and she shouldn't do business with him."

Brett shook his head and sighed. "What Officer Macklin is trying not to say is that Victor Larabee is not who he says he is."

"What does that mean?" Maggie gasped.

"It means that he is not Faylene's nephew and that he is the tabloid reporter I was telling you about," Brett explained.

"He lied? How? Why?" Maggie rambled.

"Reporters can be sneaky," Myra said. "If they're good at what they do, it's pretty easy for them to get information."

Brett nodded. "She's right."

"But why me?"

"That remains to be seen," Brett said. "But I definitely want you to keep the restraining order."

Myra tapped the table with her finger. "Do you think he might have done something to Tanya Clemmons? I mean, is it possible that he harmed her?"

Brett sipped his cinnamon latte and nodded his head. "We are looking into that possibility, along with many others."

"What happens now?" Maggie asked after a while. "I mean, will I have to go to court and testify against him or something?"

Brett rested his hand on top of Maggie's and squeezed gently. "Let's wait and see what the prosecutor wants to do after a review of the case," he said softly. "Often times, these tabloid reporters are harmless, they just like to make themselves known. They like to be intimidating in order to get their story."

"Why would that help them? You'd think anyone in their right mind would run far, far away from someone like him."

"I don't have the answers you're looking for, Maggie." Brett rested his hand on hers.

"Okay," she said, defeated. "Well, I know this isn't related to this Victor guy or whatever his name is, but there's something I need to tell you."

She told him about her research into Tanya and her blog. She explained what she'd found about the rival blogger, the Fearless Fenster, and that fenster meant window in German. Window like the tattoo on Chester Thomas.

"Chester. What an awful name," Myra said, sipping her lemonade. "I used to know a guy with that name but thankfully, he decided to use the name Chet instead. Much more flattering."

As she finished her sentence, Ruby joined them at the table. "That's it!" She said the words so loudly, it caused everyone in the group to jump. They all stared at her. "Chester Thomas. The guy from the lake. You said he was from New York, right?"

"That's right?" Brett said, suddenly very interested. "Why?"

"Is he a junior by any chance?"

"Why Ruby? What are you getting at here?" Brett asked.

"It might be nothing, but many years ago, I almost worked with a Chet Thomas. He's from a big publisher in New York. Is it possible this Chester guy you found is related?"

"I don't know, but we're about to find out." Brett nodded to Brooks, who gave Myra a quick kiss goodbye. "Maggie, I'm sorry, but we've gotta go."

The women watched as Brett and Brooks took off out of the parking lot. Finally, Maggie spoke. "Brooks told me Chester was here on business. Can we find out somehow if he's in publishing?"

Ruby held up a finger and pulled out her phone. A moment later, she nodded. "He is."

Myra looked between Maggie and Ruby. "Is one of you going to tell me what's going on?"

Ruby glanced at the clock on the wall and sat,

taking over Brett's spot. "I believe Maggie is thinking that Chester Thomas came here to Dogwood Mountain on publishing business."

"To publish who? You? I didn't know you were working on a new cookbook." Myra beamed.

"I'm not." Ruby shook her head.

"No, not for Ruby. I think he came here to meet with Tanya."

"Tanya Clemmons? The lady who just died?" Myra asked.

"What if I'm right?" Maggie eyed Ruby. "What if Chester came here to talk to Tanya but it didn't go well? They could have met at the lake and... Oh. The trash! Didn't someone call her work trash on the blog? What if Chester had something to do with all of this and her means of retaliation was to kill him and douse him in trash?"

"That's a bit of a reach, Maggie, but I see what you're getting at. I want to keep talking this through, but I have to go," she said, looking at the clock again. "I have the candidate's forum to prepare for and I need all the time I can get. I'd much rather ignore all of this and just talk about Myra's baby all day, but responsibilities beckon."

They said their goodbyes and Ruby went on her way. They'd have time to talk more after the event tonight. Honestly, even with everything going on, Maggie was glad Dogwood Mountain Mayor Jason Savino had decided not to cancel the event. A dark cloud had settled over the election with the dead body discovered at the lake followed quickly by the murder of Tanya. But the citizens needed to hear from their elected officials. In the end he decided to hold the meeting, with the addition of added security.

Maggie rushed home after work and decided to take a nap before the meeting that night. She fought the desire to jump back on her laptop and find out everything she could about every single new person that she'd met in the last few days. She knew the tabloid reporter probably had nothing to do with this mess, but at the same time, he'd proven he'd do just about anything for a story, including terrify her for no apparent reason.

After her nap, Maggie took her time getting ready for the meeting. She hung around in the kitchen and enjoyed a cup of tea while she waited until it was time to leave. Her laptop was still on the kitchen table. While she sipped her tea, she decided to check some things out. If she happened to see something that pointed her in the direction of the nameless tabloid reporter, she promised herself she'd get to the bottom of it. Angry at herself for not getting his name,

Maggie decided to google another name that was on her mind.

Sasha Lorenzo had an extensive online presence. She had profiles on every major social media platform where she referred to herself as a true crime enthusiast.

She returned to "The Town Crier," Tanya Clemmons' blog and read through her profiles even more carefully. She found Sasha's name on nearly every post going back three years. She checked on her social media pages again. She had a number of towns under "has lived in" portion of her profiles, all within the past few years. Dogwood Mountain was the latest on the list and before that was Hunter Springs. Maggie clicked on a few links in her profile that she hadn't noticed before.

Sasha Lorenzo was an amateur true crime podcaster, author, and enthusiast. It was little wonder that she had found Tanya. They seemed to operate in similar circles. What she wondered was how their paths might have crossed. Tanya seemed eager to take on law enforcement and call out police officers and public officials whenever bad things happened.

Sasha was new to the call-out part of it. Her interests seemed to lie in storytelling, at least the interests reflected in her social media presence, but she didn't seem to do very well despite what some fans had to say. Maggie wondered when she became jaded enough to call out people in public, just as Tanya had done.

Maggie backed out of the search for Sasha Lorenzo and searched for one more thing. She checked the local obituary pages and found Tanya's name. She clicked on the page and read. Tanya had been married and divorced twice. Maggie read over the words and stopped when she got to the part that listed those who preceded her in death some eight years ago. She found the name Tammy Clemmons. Her sister.

Maggie googled the name and found a link to several articles describing the death of the woman after an accident with a drunk driver. Maggie opened a new tab and returned to "The Town Crier," where she checked the archives. She went all the way back to the very beginning posts when the blog first began.

Maggie noted that the date was about six months after the death of her sister.

CHAPTER TWELVE

Maggie arrived at city hall shortly before the meeting began. She risked having no place to sit to avoid time for too much conversation. Ruby was seated at the front of the room facing the audience. Maggie thought she looked like a natural sitting in front of the podium occupied by seated council members. She looked up and waved slightly at Maggie when she caught her eye.

Maggie spotted Brett standing in front of the exit on the far side of the room. Brooks and two other officers were stationed at the other three entrances into the large council chambers. Brett was stiff and watchful. She wondered if there was more going on that she hadn't been informed about. She took the last seat on the left side of the back row and waited.

Mayor Savino walked across the front of the room and shook hands with various people. Ruby and the rest of the candidates made small talk while they waited for the meeting to begin. Maggie sat still and watched. She watched as several people came in and out of the doors. She could see even more people gathered in the foyer to her left. She wondered how many more might be coming. It was a good turnout, she thought. At least election day looked promising.

The mayor stood at the front of the room and announced that the meeting would begin in five minutes. He asked for those in attendance to find their seats so that the meeting could begin on time. The din of the room hushed immediately. Maggie felt the whoosh of air from the door closest to her seat. She spotted Sasha Lorenzo out among the crowd in the foyer.

She wondered if Victor Larabee had been released from jail. She forgot to check in with Brett and ask. Her heart raced a bit at the thought. Could he show up there tonight? The thought made her antsy. She glanced around the room. No sign of him. Maggie sat back in her chair and breathed a sigh of relief. She wanted to get through the meeting without the fear of another interaction with him.

Mayor Savino moved to the front again. He

tapped slightly on the microphone at the center podium and the crowd immediately fell silent. After a brief welcome, he announced that the meeting would begin, and asked for the members of the audience to limit their comings and goings during the meeting.

"Welcome, citizens of Dogwood Mountain, to this Meet the Candidate Forum. Tonight, you will hear from the contenders for open seats on the city council and the school board. We will begin with a discussion among the city council candidates, followed by the school board, and finally, we will have a question and answer period involving each of the participants tonight."

"Why don't we start with the question and answer period?" The shout came from the middle of the room.

"Ladies and gentlemen, we have an agenda to follow tonight." Mayor Savino returned to the podium. "Please, let us maintain order here tonight."

"I want to know what our elected officials plan to do about the crime in this community," Sasha Lorenzo shouted. She walked down the aisle separating the rows of chairs and stood ten feet from the mayor. "Not too long ago, the body of a young man was discovered at Dogwood Mountain Lake, dead.

Don't we, the public, deserve a glimpse into the window of the great police department?"

"Hold on there just a minute." Brett stepped forward. Even from far away Maggie could see the stiffness in his posture. His face reddened in frustration. "We are no longer in charge of that investigation."

"Thank you, Chief Mission, for your devotion and service to this community," Sasha said. Maggie was astonished at her demeanor and articulation. She was dressed and poised like a hot shot attorney delivering the death blow in an Orson-worthy legal drama. Gone was the bumbling woman making her ill-timed, clumsy speeches. "Do you know where the Chief was while his officers investigated the body out at the lake?"

"That is enough, Ms. Lorenzo," Brett said. "You are out of order and the mayor has already told you there will be a chance to ask your questions at the end of the night."

"Do you have that much to hide, Chief?" Sasha asked. She turned back to the people. "The night the body of young Chester Thomas was discovered at Dogwood Mountain Lake, our police chief not only met with his girlfriend and enjoyed a takeout dinner from the food truck parked in the donut shop parking lot, but she was also at the lake and found the body herself beforehand."

"Sasha Lorenzo, please take your seat and allow the meeting to run properly," Mayor Savino said. "You are disrupting this entire process."

"I am only disrupting the status quo, because this town needs to know what is going on behind closed doors," Sasha said. "Apparently, this is what it takes to make things happen."

The mayor threw his hands in the air. He gestured toward Brett. "Chief, you are going to have to restore order here," he said.

"Yes, Chief," Sasha said. "Perhaps you should do your job tonight."

"Do you know why Maggie Sharpe and I...?"

Sasha interrupted, "I'm not sure any of us really want to know what you were doing with Ms. Sharpe." She smirked.

Maggie stood up, having had entirely enough. "I was there with my son Bradley and my grandson, Wyatt. I had to stop at the restroom on the way out of the lake. That's when I discovered the body of the young man. That's why the chief and I were together. Neither of us had eaten dinner so later on, after Brett did what he had to do at the lake, we stopped at the food truck for something to eat. We discussed what I had seen when I found the body. Now, I'm sorry if that isn't salacious enough for you, but there it is."

"Well," Sasha stammered. "I saw you two out on a date together at Curley's the other night."

"We do go out together," Maggie said. "And you were vocal that night as well."

A grin spread across Sasha's face. "I was there, along with the next person who was murdered in Dogwood Mountain," she said. "Tell me, Ms. Sharpe, just how angry were you that night? Tanya Clemmons was there that night, wasn't she? And if I recall, she called you out along with the police chief. Did that make you angry? Maybe angry enough with her that you would want to shut her up?"

"I know that," Maggie said. "And I know she was your friend. It must have been tough to discover her the following day."

Sasha stammered again. "Tanya Clemmons wasn't my friend," she said. "I had just met her. But we had something in common. Not only were we both new to town, but she was a diehard advocate for community safety and so was I. When I met her, she was fighting the good fight here in this town. And that is more than you, the police, or any of these politicians have ever done!"

Maggie glanced over at Brett. "You weren't old

friends with Tanya, then?" she asked, beginning to piece things together. "I was under the impression you and Tanya Clemmons went way back."

"Can we be done with this conversation?" Mayor Savino asked. "There are nine people on this panel and a room filled with citizens waiting to hear from them."

"Not yet," Maggie said, apologizing to Brett with her eyes. She had to shoot her shot and knew it the minute she heard Sasha say the town deserved a glimpse into the window of the police department. "Sasha, you said yourself that you and Tanya had something in common. From what I've read on your blog and hers, it seems that your commonality lay in more than simple activism."

"What's that supposed to mean?" Sasha scoffed and looked around the room.

"I know Tanya was trying to get her books noticed. Is that true for you as well? I noticed you have a knack for storytelling." Maggie gave her own smirk.

Sasha stood with her mouth agape.

"Is it true that you were so angry with Chester Thomas for agreeing to a meeting with Tanya about her books that you killed him?"

"What! No!" Sasha's face turned red.

Now Maggie felt like a hot shot attorney. "Is it true that you not only killed him, but piled trash all over his body to make it look like Tanya might have done it?" Everyone in the room had their full attention on Maggie. "And then you killed Tanya to finish it all off? You see, you probably could have gotten away with Chester. It might have made sense, maybe he denied Tanya what she wanted for her books. But by killing Tanya, you ruined it for yourself."

"You have no idea what you're talking about. Tanya and I weren't friends, but that doesn't mean I was jealous of her!"

"Okay, so tell me this. How did you two both end up in Dogwood Mountain? Which one of you moved here first?" Maggie waited all of three seconds before she kept going. "I'm betting you followed her here because you wanted to know why she was getting traction being more of a vocal activist. You did well for yourself, and it was obvious that her readers thought more of you than her, but you couldn't figure out why she was getting her stories into books."

"Her books were trash!" Sasha shouted. "Have you seen those covers?" She slapped her hand over her mouth.

Maggie smiled. "They might have been amateur, but they were selling, and you were furious that

someone was interested in giving her more of a platform. You wanted that for yourself, didn't you? You
commented hundreds of times on Tanya's blog, you
followed her here, and you couldn't handle seeing her
potential success, so you did what you had to do."
She crossed her arms. "Tell me I'm wrong. I'll wait."

"No need to wait," Brett interrupted. He walked
across the front of the room and pulled out a pair of
handcuffs. Brooks Macklin walked up the center aisle
toward her.

"What are you doing?" Sasha said. "What's
going on?"

"Sasha Lorenzo, you need to come with us."

"What?" Mayor Savino headed straight for the
police chief. Brett gripped Sasha by the arm and held
her until Brooks was able to reach her. He leaned over
and whispered in the mayor's ear.

The mayor stepped back and nodded to the crowd.

"Ladies and gentlemen, we are going to take a
five minute break after which we will reconvene the
town hall meeting," he said. "Please stand back while
the Dogwood Mountain Police Department does what
they need to do."

CHAPTER THIRTEEN

Ruby held the wine glass high in the air. "To election night," she said. "And to the Dogwood Mountain Police Department for apprehending yet another dangerous criminal."

Maggie raised her glass. Brett leaned over and winked at her while Ruby spoke. They were seated in their usual places, watching the flames spark and pop in the bonfire while they waited for the results to start trickling in. The polls had closed just over an hour before. It was nice being able to sit with friends and enjoy the night.

"I would like to add another toast," Brett said. He was seated in the Adirondack chair next to Maggie's. His hand rested just centimeters from hers. He leaned in slightly as he spoke. "Once more, our local amateur sleuth assisted in the apprehension of that dangerous suspect. Here's to Maggie Sharpe and her inability to leave well enough alone."

Myra shifted in her seat. "I'm still not clear on how you knew Sasha Lorenzo was the murderer," she said. "One minute she is standing up at that town hall meeting raising all kinds of heck with Brett and Maggie and the city itself, and the next minute my husband has her in handcuffs and is walking her out of city hall."

"Tanya's community activism blog, 'The Town Crier,'" Maggie said. "I read through many, many posts. And what I found was something of a fangirl in Sasha. She practically stalked Tanya Clemmons."

"Then why did she kill her?" Myra asked.

"For a lot of reasons, probably. But I figured it out with the little keywords that people tend to miss unless they're really paying attention. Like, I knew Fearless Fenster was Tanya's rival, but because of the tattoo on Chester, it led me to believe it was him. I wasn't completely sure about anything until I heard Sasha use the word window. Then I thought of how someone had called Tanya's books trash and Chester just happened to be covered in trash. I definitely didn't know if I was right but there were way too many signs that I was. Sasha followed Tanya here to see why she was getting her stories into books. Sasha might have had the backing from the fans on Tanya's blog, but that wasn't enough for her. She wanted more. That and I knew they had to know each other. Sasha tried to lie and say they'd just met. That might have been true physically, but they went way back online."

"Anything for a story," Orson huffed, repeating what Maggie had said several times before.

"I began looking into Sasha after that night at Curley's," Brett added "And Brooks did some internet sleuthing of his own after we heard from Maggie about Sasha's apparent obsession with Tanya Clemmons. We got to wondering what the nature of their relationship might have been, given the fact that Sasha is the one who discovered Tanya and reported her death."

"And when she denied that she was friends with Tanya, or claimed that she barely knew her, that solidified our theory about her," Brooks said to his wife. "Sasha acted like a bumbling buffoon around Tanya in order to get close to whatever cause she was working on at the moment. She did the same thing in Kansas, which is where Tanya began her activism."

"Sasha was a podcaster and a wannabe true crime

author," Brett continued. "On the surface, she was a dismal failure. But, as you saw that night at city hall, she was also a bit of a chameleon."

"She put on a good act in order to pirate a good story for her blog and her podcast," Ruby said. "What I don't understand is how she was able to garner any following at all. From her social media profiles, she wasn't a very popular podcaster."

"Not on the surface," Maggie said. "But we found out that Sasha Lorenzo wasn't the only name she used online."

Ruby set her wine glass down and gawked at Maggie. "It was her, wasn't it," she said suddenly. "Sasha Lorenzo was the other blogger everyone on Tanya's blog compared her to. Not poor Chester. He just was unlucky enough to have the wrong tattoo."

"And recommended over her," Maggie said. "As soon as Sasha began speaking at the candidate's forum, I knew she had been putting on a huge act for everyone else to see."

"You should have heard her that night at the Italian restaurant. There was nothing similar to the way she acted that night and the performance she gave in front of the entire town," Brett said. "Along with her denial of knowing Tanya, it was the confirmation we needed to make the arrest."

"I'm still not entirely clear of her motive," Myra admitted. "If she was this infamous blogger person why kill Tanya Clemmons? Why kill anyone if you have a good thing going?"

"Whatever she called herself, her ego got bruised a few too many times by Tanya Clemmons," Brett explained. "And Tanya herself was starting to gain more momentum as an activist."

"Did anyone ever figure out why Victor, I mean.. wait, what is his name?" Maggie asked.

"Seth Silverton. It turns out that Tanya had contacted him to come to town and prove her theory about the local police," Brett replied. "As you all know, she didn't have a whole lot of faith in small town police departments so when she caught wind that Maggie here does a bit of her own investigating…"

"She thought bringing in this Seth guy would prove her right, all while making us look like fools? Maggie finished. "I couldn't figure out what he wanted with me. This whole time, he just wanted to what? Prove that I was helping to solve a few cases? That's hardly newsworthy."

"I knew that guy wasn't to be trusted. I can sense these things from a mile away," Orson grumbled.

Brett's cell phone rang then. He picked it up and

stepped away from the circle of chairs and walked toward the house. All eyes followed him as he walked and listened to the speaker on the other end of the line. When the conversation was over, he pocketed the phone and walked somberly back to the bonfire.

"Were those election results?" Maggie asked, looking over at Orson who was swelling with pride and excitement.

Brett nodded his head. "Jason Savino just called to let me know the results," he said.

"Well? Don't keep us in suspense," Orson said. "Do we have a new city council person, at large?"

Brett nodded his head slowly. "With one hundred percent of the votes counted. It was a landslide. Ruby Cobb, you are the newest member of city council with eighty percent of the vote."

Maggie stood and hugged her best friend. Brooks, Myra, Orson, and Brett raised their glasses to her again in congratulations.

"Well, Madam City councilperson, what do you have to say for yourself?" Brett asked.

Ruby stood and raised her own glass to her friends. "First of all, thank you to my friends for your support and belief that I could do this," she said. "But I have to say, after the events of the past few days,

I'm starting to wonder what I may have just gotten myself into."

***

If you enjoyed Cruller Me Surprised, check out the next book in the series, Easy Come Easy Dough, today!

AUTHOR'S NOTE

I'd love to hear your thoughts on my books, the storylines, and anything else that you'd like to comment on—reader feedback is very important to me. My contact information, along with some other helpful links, is listed on the next page. If you'd like to be on my list of "folks to contact" with updates, release and sales notifications, etc.… just shoot me an email and let me know. Thanks for reading!

Also…

… if you're looking for more great reads, Summer Prescott Books publishes several popular series by outstanding Cozy Mystery authors.

CONTACT SUMMER PRESCOTT BOOKS PUBLISHING

Blog and Book Catalog: http://summerprescottbooks.com

Email: summer.prescott.cozies@gmail.com

And...be sure to check out the Summer Prescott Cozy Mysteries fan page and Summer Prescott Books Publishing Page on Facebook – let's be friends!

To sign up for our fun and exciting newsletter, which will give you opportunities to win prizes and swag, enter contests, and be the first to know about New Releases, click here: http://summerprescottbooks.com

Made in United States
North Haven, CT
15 March 2023